PUFFIN BOOKS

DIARY OF A WIMPY KID

THE *DIARY OF A WIMPY KID* SERIES

MORE FROM THE *WIMPY* WORLD

DIARY
of a
Wimpy Kid

Hot Mess

by Jeff Kinney

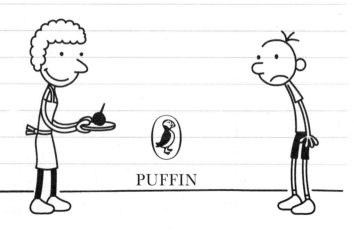

PUFFIN

PUFFIN BOOKS

UK | USA | Canada | Ireland | Australia

India | New Zealand | South Africa

Puffin Books is part of the Penguin Random House group of companies
whose addresses can be found at global.penguinrandomhouse.com.

www.penguin.co.uk   www.puffin.co.uk   www.ladybird.co.uk

First published in the USA by Amulet Books, an imprint of ABRAMS, 2024.
All rights reserved.
First published in Great Britain by Puffin Books 2024

001

Printed and bound in Great Britain by Clays Ltd, Elcograf S.p.A.

The authorized representative in the EEA is Penguin Random House Ireland,
Morrison Chambers, 32 Nassau Street, Dublin DO2 YH68

A CIP catalogue record for this book is available from the British Library

ISBN: 978-0-241-58316-6

All correspondence to:
Puffin Books, Penguin Random House Children's
One Embassy Gardens, 8 Viaduct Gardens, London SW11 7BW

TO PAUL-ANTHONY

<u>Monday</u>

My dad's always saying you can pick your nose, but you can't pick your family. And even though I get his meaning, it doesn't exactly make me want to share a bowl of popcorn with him.

He's right about family, though. Because the second you're born, you're automatically in a group of people you never asked to be a part of.

In fact, when you're born, a BUNCH of stuff has already been decided for you, like where you'll live and even what language you'll speak. But since you can't actually TALK yet, you can't tell the people taking care of you that mushed-up prunes and carrots are a bad combination.

The first thing you learn as a kid is that grown-ups are the ones in charge. And the SECOND thing you learn is that they don't always make the best decisions.

Then you find out that the people in charge of YOU have people who are in charge of THEM.

At least that's the way it is in my family, where Gramma's the one who calls the shots. But you'd never know she had so much power just by looking at her.

I MADE YOU YOUR FAVORITE COOKIES!

There's actually a whole story to how Gramma became the head of our family.

When my great grandmother Meemaw passed away, someone needed to step up to take her place as our leader. But since Gramma was the youngest of four sisters, it didn't look like she'd be the one to take over the family.

But then something happened that changed all that. For Easter brunch one year, Gramma made a pot of meatballs, and everyone went CRAZY for them.

Great Uncle Herman declared that Gramma was the best cook in the family. Everybody else agreed, which I'm sure was hard for her older sisters.

The way it works in my family is that if you're the best cook, you get to host the big holidays like Thanksgiving and Christmas. But Gramma's older sisters all live far away, and they don't like to travel on the holidays.

So Great Aunt Lou came up with a special recipe of her OWN to try and one-up Gramma, but she just couldn't top Gramma's meatballs.

Ever since Gramma introduced her special meatballs, everyone's been trying to get her to tell them the secret recipe.

But Gramma's no dummy. She knows that giving it up would be giving up her POWER.

So she just tells everybody that her meatballs
only have one ingredient, and it's "love."

Nobody seems satisfied with that answer,
though, and lately a few of my aunts have been
trying to STEAL the recipe.

Last Christmas, Aunt Gretchen tried to sneak
away with a few meatballs so she could take
them to a lab and get them analyzed for their
ingredients. The only reason she didn't get away
with it was because Gramma's dog, Sweetie, sniffed
them out before she could get to her car.

Then, one night, Aunt Audra came to stay with Gramma and hid her phone in a kitchen cabinet so she could record Gramma making a batch of meatballs. But Gramma discovered the hidden phone and put it in the garbage disposal.

Everybody's always telling Gramma her recipe is so good, she should open a restaurant and make a pile of money. My Aunt Veronica is a businesswoman, and she even came up with a plan for a whole CHAIN of restaurants that would serve Gramma's meatballs.

But Gramma shut that idea down by saying that you can't get a real home-cooked meal in a restaurant, and her meatballs were only for the family.

I don't mean to sound harsh or anything, but I hope Gramma shares her recipe with someone in the family SOON, because she's not getting any younger. In fact, she just moved out of her house and into an assisted living center a few miles away.

Mom says Gramma's happy there because she's with people her age and they have lots of activities. But I sure hope my kids don't try and ship ME off to a place like that when I'm old, because I'm actually looking forward to being a burden to my children.

Gramma's turning seventy-five soon, and my mom and her sisters told Gramma they wanted to throw a big party for her birthday. But Gramma says she doesn't want anyone to go to any trouble for her, and she doesn't have the energy for a party like that anymore.

Then Gramma said what would make her REALLY happy is if everyone else went to Ruttyneck Island, where the family used to vacation back when Mom and her sisters were kids.

Gramma said the only gift she wanted was a photo of the whole family on the beach with the old lighthouse in the background, like the picture she keeps in her apartment.

I guess Mom and her sisters couldn't say no to Gramma's birthday request because they'd feel too guilty.

So just like that, everybody's summer plans got turned upside down, which proves Gramma is the one pulling the strings in our family.

I'm not looking forward to this trip, though, because I'm really not a beach person. But Mom says we'll make happy family memories, and she even booked the same house they stayed in as kids to make the vacation extra special.

From the picture, the beach house looks a little small to me, and there are a whole lot more people in the family now than there were when Mom and her sisters were young. But what I'm really nervous about is the combination of people going on vacation together.

Mom and her sisters only see each other a few times a year, and there's a reason for that. Whenever they're together, all they do is FIGHT. And sometimes it gets so bad between them that Gramma has to step in to break things up.

So I want to say for the record that this whole trip is a bad idea. The way I see it, a family vacation is like a recipe, and some ingredients just don't mix.

Tuesday

Mom's been trying to get me and my brothers excited by showing us old photo albums from her family vacations on Ruttyneck Island. But every so often, there's a page where someone was cut out of a picture.

Mom explained that if one of my aunts dated some boy and they broke up, Gramma would cut them out of the photo. That's because she feels like family photo albums are only for FAMILY.

All of a sudden, something I always used to wonder about made sense. When I was little, I found an envelope stuffed with cutouts of teenagers, and I never knew who they were.

I'd play with them like they were action figures, and I created these crazy storylines for each character.

The last time Mom's family went to Ruttyneck Island, she and her sisters were in high school. Aunt Cakey must've had a boyfriend that summer, because there were a bunch of pictures of her next to someone who'd been cut out.

But when I asked Mom about Aunt Cakey's boyfriend, she said it was a long time ago and she couldn't remember anything about him.

I guess Gramma got sick of cutting ex-boyfriends out of photos, because eventually she made a rule that you're not allowed to be in family pictures unless you've officially married in.

And that's a little awkward for Vincent, who's been dating Aunt Cakey for six years but always has to stand behind the camera when we take our family photos.

Whitehead Library

libraries ni
www.librariesni.org.uk

17B Edward Road
Whitehead
Antrim
BT38 9QB

Customer ID: ******4775

Items that you have checked out

Title: Fly who told a lie
ID: C904474928
Due: 18 February 2025

Title: Hot mess
ID: C904448930
Due: 18 February 2025

Title: Three little pigs
ID: C904476114
Due: 18 February 2025

Total items: 3
Account balance: £0.00
Checked out: 3
Overdue: 0
Hold requests: 0
Ready for collection: 0
28/01/2025 10:37

t: 028 93353249
e: whitehead.library@librariesni.org.uk

We learned our lesson about this kind of thing by taking too many pictures of Noah, who dated Aunt Veronica for a while. Everybody in the family LOVED Noah, and he was front and center in a lot of our pictures.

In fact, a couple of times, he even made it into our family newsletter that Gramma mails out every year.

The Family Follies

NOAH DOES IT AGAIN!

Promoted to Regional Manager

What will Noah do next?

Unfortunately, it didn't work out between Noah and Aunt Veronica, so he vanished from the family newsletter. And that made things kind of awkward whenever our family would run into someone who was on the mailing list.

But what was even MORE awkward was when Gramma found out Noah still had a T-shirt from our family reunion, and she went to his gym to make him give it BACK.

I think Vincent's planning on proposing to Aunt Cakey one day, and he knows he needs to get Gramma's blessing first. He's been working hard to impress her, but I can tell she's gonna milk this as long as she can.

To be honest, I really don't understand why Vincent's so eager to be a part of our family. In fact, if he wants MY slot, I'd be happy to just hand it to him.

And I don't know if there are lawyers or paperwork involved in that kind of a deal, but I'd be willing to do whatever it takes to get this thing done.

Wednesday

Even though I'm not looking forward to spending a week at the beach with my family, there's one thing I AM excited about doing, and that's going out to eat.

Mom says Ruttyneck Island has a bunch of restaurants, and I'm planning on eating at a different one every night.

At home, we almost NEVER go out to eat, and when we do, it's almost always to a family-style restaurant like Corny's. So I'm looking forward to going to a restaurant where they don't use a garden hose to clean off your table.

FWOOSH

It would also be nice to go to a place where you eat off a plate instead of from a BUCKET.

But I'm kind of worried about how my family might behave at a classy restaurant, because the last time we ate at a fancy place, it didn't go well.

We went out for dinner to celebrate Mom getting her master's degree, and the restaurant had white linen tablecloths. But my family is used to going to places like Corny's, where the tablecloths are made of paper and you can draw on them with crayons and markers.

And before anyone realized what he was doing, Manny had covered his end of the table with drawings.

I guess those fancy tablecloths are expensive, because the restaurant made my parents pay for it. But Mom decided that if we had to pay for the tablecloth, that meant we OWNED it, so we took it home with us. And now we pull it out every time we have a special meal.

But whenever one of my cousins comes to our house, they write on the tablecloth. And the last time Aunt Gretchen's family came to visit, one of her twins wrote a bad word in six-inch letters in permanent marker.

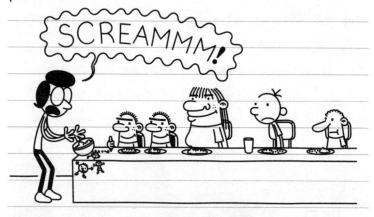

This thing with the tablecloth never would've happened if the members of my family just knew how to act CIVILIZED.

My friend Rowley's family eats at their country club at least once a week, so they know how you're supposed to act at a fancy restaurant. But when the Jeffersons invited me to come along with them one time, I had no idea how you were supposed to behave in a place like that.

First of all, I'm used to going to places where there are pictures of the different menu items, and you just point at what you want to order.

But at the country club, there weren't any pictures, and the menu was all in FRENCH. So when Rowley ordered, I thought it sounded kind of goofy.

The restaurant also had expensive silverware, and there was a different type of fork for each course, which seemed a little silly to me.

I'm just glad we're living in a time where the fork is what we use to eat, because it wasn't all that long ago that people actually used DAGGERS to feed themselves. And it's stressful enough in the cafeteria at my school as it is.

There are certain types of food you wouldn't even be able to eat without a fork. And good luck to anyone trying to eat spaghetti with a knife.

I wish I'd never learned to master the fork, though. When I was a baby, I really enjoyed being fed by someone else.

Once you learn to feed yourself, everyone expects you to KEEP doing it. But I'm looking forward to the day when I can free up my hands while I'm eating again.

The menus and the silverware weren't the only things that were different about the country club.

At Corny's, the waiters wear cowboy hats and overalls with holes in them. But at the country club, the waiters were dressed in tuxedos and looked like they were going to a wedding.

Each server had a different thing they were in charge of. There was even one guy whose whole job was to use a knife to scrape crumbs off the tablecloth. And I made sure to create LOTS of crumbs so that guy felt like he was earning his money.

They even had people working in the BATHROOM. One guy's job was to hand you a little towel to dry your hands after you washed them, which seemed a little odd to me. In fact, at first, I didn't even realize that he was a restaurant employee.

I thought he was just some random person who was hanging out near the sink, which is why I reported him to the manager.

For an appetizer, the waiter brought us bowls of soup. I don't know what was IN it, but it was really delicious.

I remembered reading that in some countries, the way you show your appreciation to your server is by slurping your soup. But I got the feeling that's not the way you're supposed to do things at the Jeffersons' country club.

SLURRRP

When it came time to order the main course, I couldn't believe how EXPENSIVE everything was. I tried to convince Mr. and Mrs. Jefferson to just give me the money they would've spent on my meal instead, because there was a lot I could do with that kind of cash.

But Mr. Jefferson told me not to worry about how much things cost and to pick something from the menu I thought I'd enjoy.

I couldn't decide between lobster tail and steak, though, so I ordered BOTH.

The main course took a long time to come, and while we were waiting for our dinner, the waiter kept refilling our breadstick basket. So by the time my two main courses arrived, I was totally STUFFED.

I'm hoping that there's a restaurant like that on Ruttyneck Island, because I don't feel like I've had the full fancy dining experience yet. Hopefully, when I get home, the Jeffersons will invite me back to their country club, because there were a few items on the dessert menu that looked like they were to DIE for.

<u>Saturday</u>

Mom said her favorite part of her family vacations to Ruttyneck Island was the ferry ride over. But that was the thing I was dreading the MOST.

First of all, I've heard stories about killer whales randomly attacking boats. And that doesn't sound like a great way to kick off a vacation to me.

But the thing I was even MORE nervous about was PIRATES, because Mom said that back in the old days, Ruttyneck Island was a notorious pirate hideout.

Dad said it's been a long time since pirates sailed the seas around these parts, but I was worried that there could still be a few stragglers who never got the message to quit. And those guys are gonna be pretty ticked off when they realize they've been missing out on things like cell phones and soft-serve ice cream all these years.

Whenever you see a movie about pirates, there's always some kid on board whose job is to swab the decks or climb up into the crow's nest to be on the lookout for other ships. But I'd be totally USELESS in a job like that.

I have a fear of heights, so I couldn't work as a lookout. I'd get seasick if I had to mop the deck while the ship was moving, and I'm pretty sure I'd be lousy at playing the fife. So they'd probably toss me overboard after a day or two.

I figure the kids on those ships didn't CHOOSE to be pirates, which means they were kidnapped. And ever since I was little, I've been worried that could happen to ME.

When I turned six years old, my mother booked a harbor cruise for my birthday as a surprise.

But when I saw the boat waiting at the dock, I had a total meltdown.

So Mom got tickets for a boat that DIDN'T have a pirate theme, and I thought we were safe. But the pirate cruise caught up with us in the harbor, and I spent the rest of my birthday walking around in wet clothes.

There are other things to worry about besides whales and pirates, though. We just wrapped up our unit on Greek mythology in school, and the thing those stories make clear is that the gods don't like people going where they don't belong.

So before we stepped on the ferry this afternoon, I took a minute to show some proper respect.

OH MIGHTY POSEIDON, PLEASE GRANT ME SAFE PASSAGE INTO YOUR KINGDOM!

TO FERRY

At first, it was smooth sailing. But when the wind picked up in the middle of the ride and the waves got choppy, I was pretty nervous we might capsize.

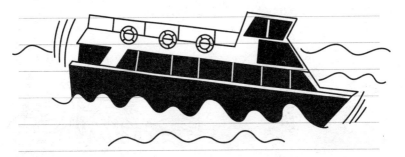

It was so rocky that half the people on board got sick. In fact, there were so many people throwing up overboard that I was afraid I might do it MYSELF.

BLECH!

I went inside to get away from everyone on deck. But the main cabin was like a hospital ward, which meant there was no place for me to escape.

The ferry ride was only three hours, but it felt more like three DAYS. And when we finally safely reached the shore, there was no one happier to be on dry land than ME.

Welcome to
RUTTYNECK
ISLAND

KISS KISS

We took a cab into town, which turned out to be a mistake. There were so many pedestrians clogging the road that we couldn't even move, and nobody seemed concerned they were blocking traffic.

RUTTYNECK TAXI

Mom was getting anxious about how long it was taking, because the sun was going down and it was starting to get dark. Plus, she had the only key and she wanted to get to the house before her sisters did.

So after sitting in traffic for half an hour, she decided she'd had enough.

We took our suitcases out of the trunk and walked the mile and a half to our beach house, which wasn't easy with all the stuff we were carrying.

On top of that, Mom didn't seem to know where she was going. I guess there'd been a lot of development on the island since she was here with her family on their last trip, and it took her a long time to find the beach house where they used to stay.

Mom took out the key to unlock the door, but
it was cracked open. And we were surprised to
discover that Aunt Gretchen and her twins were
inside and had already made themselves at home.

Aunt Gretchen said they got there a half hour
earlier, and since the door was locked, they crawled
in through the bathroom window. Then they put their
stuff in the biggest bedroom, which Mom had been
reserving for OUR family.

I guess Mom didn't want to start the trip with a fight, so she just let Aunt Gretchen's family have the master bedroom. But the next-biggest room was already occupied by Aunt Veronica and her dog, Dazzle, who were both in the middle of a nap after a long day of traveling.

I was surprised that Aunt Veronica made the trip, since she lives in the city with her dog, and the two of them almost never leave their apartment. That's because Dazzle is famous, and she can't really go out in public anymore.

The way it happened is a little nuts. Aunt Veronica makes videos for the internet telling people how to invest their money. And sometimes Dazzle would walk through the background while Aunt Veronica was live streaming.

But once her followers started noticing the dog, that's all they wanted to see.

FINANCIAL PLANNING WITH VERONICA

Comments
jmarquis89star> There it is again!
hiphobknob98> What breed is that?
moneymattrz> Apricot pug I think.
home^Mkr> OMG I need one!

Aunt Veronica saw an opportunity, so she dropped the whole investment advice thing and just made videos about her pet. And within a year, Dazzle had 3.7 million followers and a line of merchandise that people can purchase online.

It turns out that when you've got millions of followers, companies will send you free products so that you use them in your videos. After a while, Dazzle got so much free stuff that Aunt Veronica had to move to a bigger apartment just to handle everything that was coming in.

But being a social media star comes with a lot of pressure, too. Aunt Veronica has to film Dazzle around the clock, because when she's not streaming, she feels like she's losing money.

I guess Aunt Veronica decided she couldn't do it all by herself anymore, though, so she hired a whole team of people to help her. And before long, Dazzle had a groomer, a photographer, a videographer, and one person whose only job was to keep the dog's nose wet.

But fame's got a dark side, because people started showing up outside Aunt Veronica's apartment to get a glimpse of Dazzle.

But that's not gonna be easy. Right before the trip started, Aunt Veronica posted a fake picture of Dazzle in front of the Eiffel Tower to throw Dazzle's followers off her trail. But Aunt Veronica was a little sloppy with her photo editing, which is why the dog ended up with five paws.

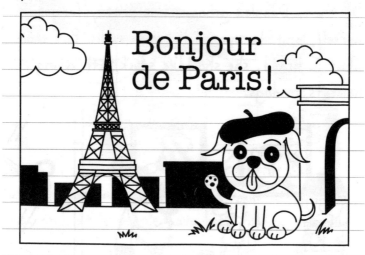

So now everyone on the internet has a theory about what's going on with the dog, and they're more curious about her than ever.

fitR4ven> Five paws!
g1bbonz> I saw that too! ◯◯
sn00kky> What are they trying to hide?
sussKinz> PREGNANT?

Personally, I think the whole social media thing is a little crazy. There's one guy online who films himself unboxing kitchen appliances, and he got so many followers he was able to quit his day job.

Back in olden times, people had lots of kids so they could work on the family farm. But if I ever have kids of my own, I'm gonna put them to work being social media influencers. And the second they're born, they're gonna have a camera in their face.

The only reason I haven't tried becoming an influencer myself is because I don't have a phone. And that's pretty embarrassing, because both of my cousins have one, and they're not even out of elementary school yet.

Mom thinks Aunt Gretchen's twins are too young to have phones of their own and that they're on electronics way too much. But Aunt Gretchen thinks Mom is overprotective, and once the two of them start arguing about this topic, there's no stopping them.

Aunt Gretchen accuses Mom of being a "helicopter parent" who's always hovering over us kids. But even though Aunt Gretchen might be right about that, I've always LIKED having a helicopter mom nearby to keep me safe.

In fact, Mom's saved me from a BUNCH of situations where I could've gotten myself seriously injured.

But maybe I've gotten a little TOO used to my mom having my back. Because sometimes I get a little nervous crossing the street without help from a grown-up.

Even though Mom can be a little overprotective, Aunt Gretchen lets Malcolm and Malvin do whatever they want. And I think a little parenting would go a long way with those two.

Speaking of being overprotective, Aunt Veronica treats Dazzle like she's her child. In fact, I'm pretty sure Dazzle thinks she's an actual human being, and Aunt Veronica gets touchy when you use certain phrases around her.

I'M DOG-TIRED AFTER THAT TRIP!

GASP

Aunt Veronica thinks that if Dazzle realizes she's an animal, she won't be able to handle it. The first thing Aunt Veronica did when she got to the beach house was cover up all the mirrors and shiny surfaces, so the dog wouldn't see her own reflection. Unfortunately, that's gonna make it hard for everyone to use the toaster.

I don't think it's fair to make Dazzle think she's a human being, because she's bound to find out the truth one day. I'll bet Tarzan got really messed up thinking he was an ape, especially during his teenage years.

Aunt Veronica might be a little quirky, but she's nothing compared to my Aunt Audra, who showed up at the house a half hour after we did. And she didn't waste any time before she started acting like her kooky self.

At least Mom gets along with Aunt Audra, because she's not that way with Aunt Cakey, who arrived a few minutes later. And I can always tell Mom and Aunt Cakey are being mean to each other even when they're pretending to be nice.

It seems like there's something ELSE going on between Mom and Aunt Cakey that would explain why they don't get along. But every time I ask Mom what the deal is with the two of them, Mom always changes the subject.

The only person Aunt Cakey treats worse than Mom is DAD, so it's pretty obvious he must've done something to set her off at some point.

I can tell Dad doesn't love being around Mom and her sisters when they're all together. And when he found out about the trip, he tried to get out of it by saying things are really busy at work.

But Mom said Gramma wanted us to be together, and besides, Dad needed to be there for the family picture.

52

If I ever get married, it's gonna be to someone who's an only child. Because you're not just marrying a person, you're marrying their entire FAMILY.

Aunt Cakey claimed the last bedroom with a king-sized bed, and Aunt Audra took the room with the queen. That meant my parents had to sleep on the bunk beds, which they didn't seem too thrilled about.

But they should be glad they got beds to sleep in at ALL, because the rest of us had to scramble for what we could find. Vincent found a cot in a closet and set it up in the hallway between the kitchen and the bathroom.

Manny made a nest with blankets in a dresser drawer in the living room, and Rodrick found a portable crib in the pantry that he set up in the living room. I couldn't see how he could sleep in a playpen, but the second he laid down, he was out like a light.

That left me with the couch, and at first I thought I hit the jackpot. But that thing smelled like sweat and suntan lotion and feet, and who knows HOW many farts have gotten trapped in those cushions over the years.

So I put a blanket on the floor and used a throw
pillow from the couch. But I guess Vincent couldn't
fall asleep, because he came into the living room and
watched a reality TV show with the volume at full
blast.

Eventually, Vincent went back to his cot, so I
got up and turned off the TV. I started to
fall asleep, but I'd forgotten all about Malcolm
and Malvin, who had gone on a snack run.

They turned on the lights in the kitchen, which woke up everyone in the living room.

So this trip's off to a rough start. And if this vacation is anything like that reality TV show, I'd be happy to vote MYSELF off the island.

<u>Sunday</u>

Mom woke everyone up this morning bright and early. I don't know how anyone else slept, but I felt like I'd been sleeping on a brick.

And that's because I kind of HAD been. One of the twins swiped my throw pillow in the middle of the night and replaced it with a BOOK, which wouldn't have been so bad if it wasn't a hardcover.

My plan was to hang back at the house and get a few more hours of sleep while everybody else went off and did their thing. But Mom said it was important for the family to do everything TOGETHER on this vacation, and she told us all to get ready for a day at the beach.

Like I said, I'm not really a beach person, but I figured I could just lay low and take a nap under the umbrella. So we had a quick breakfast, packed up our stuff, and headed down there.

When Mom told us about the beach house, I thought it was actually ON the beach. But we had to haul all our gear there, which wasn't a lot of fun.

Mom put me in charge of the cooler, which was heavy because it was packed with stuff like sandwiches and water bottles. It wasn't so bad pulling it when we were walking on the road because it was on wheels.

But the wheels were pretty useless once we got to the beach, where they dug into the sand.

To make matters worse, we had to walk all the way around this big taped-off area that was a nesting spot for piping plovers, which Aunt Audra explained are endangered. According to her, there are only a few thousand plovers in the world, and this beach is one of the only protected habitats left.

With all that space being taken up by birds, it didn't leave much room for us humans. So it took a while to find a spot that was big enough for our stuff.

Mom told me I needed to put on sunscreen, but I already took care of that back at the house. Because when it comes to protecting my skin, I don't mess around.

The more time you spend out in the sun, the older you look later on. And my goal is to be one of those grandpas who looks great for their age.

Even when I've got my skin slathered in sunscreen, I try to stay in the shade as much as possible. But that's not always easy, especially when your family only has one beach umbrella.

Back in the old days, people used to carry around these little umbrellas called parasols, so they took their shade WITH them. And sometimes I feel like I was born in the wrong era, because from the paintings I've seen of that period, those people really knew how to LIVE.

The other thing those guys had right were their bathing suits, which covered up a lot. Because these days when you go to the beach, there's just a little too much skin for my taste.

I've noticed that the more fit a person is, the fewer clothes they wear. And if I ever get in shape, believe me, I'm gonna be the exact same way.

Once everyone got settled, Mom tried to get us to join her down at the water for a swim. But I already decided before we got here that I wasn't going swimming on this trip, for a BUNCH of reasons.

For starters, in the ocean, you can't see through the water, which means you never know what's under the surface.

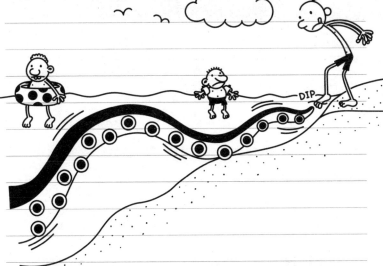

And even though Mom told me there hasn't been a shark attack on Ruttyneck Island in a hundred years, I don't wanna be the one to break the streak.

Mom always says that sharks are misunderstood, and that they're not really a threat to humans. But all you need to do is take one look at how many teeth a shark has in its mouth to know that they're made for one purpose, and that's BITING.

The only GOOD thing about sharks is that they've got a fin on their back that pops out of the water, so at least you know when one is coming. Or at least MOST of the time you do.

But if a shark somehow gets born WITHOUT a fin one day, it's gonna be bad news for us humans. So I'm just hoping sharks don't suddenly mutate into the no-fin variety.

I learned about evolution in science class, and how animals adapt with mutations.

Anteaters used to have short noses, and then one was randomly born with a LONG one. It was easier for that guy to get at the ants deep in their anthills, which meant it could get more food. And after that, the short-nosed anteaters got left in the dust.

The same sort of thing might happen with human beings, and somebody could be born with some weird change that gives them an advantage over everyone ELSE.

But sometimes it takes millions of years for there to be even a small change in a species, which means I won't live long enough to see it happen. So I've been exposing myself to lots of gamma rays to hurry things along.

This kid at school named Albert Sandy always says that one day people are gonna develop gills so they can breathe underwater. And even though that sounds kind of awesome, I hope it doesn't happen to me FIRST, because the bullying would be pretty terrible.

If we need to live underwater one day, I'm gonna have to wear a wet suit full-time. My skin gets wrinkly after twenty minutes in the bathtub, so I can't imagine what it would look like after a week of living in the ocean.

Living underwater might not be that bad, actually. For one thing, nobody will get bent out of shape about the small stuff, like juice spills.

But if the ocean is our future home, we need to start treating it better. And it's not too hard to see why sharks are always biting people.

Something that annoys me is that Aunt Gretchen ENCOURAGES her twins to pee in the ocean. At least, I'm just hoping that's ALL they're doing in there.

Even if I DID want to swim in the ocean today, I wouldn't feel safe doing it. The lifeguards are all teenagers, and I wouldn't put my life in the hands of someone who isn't even allowed to vote.

Dad used to be a lifeguard back when he was a teenager, so he's been trying to get Rodrick to earn his lifesaving certificate. But it's kind of hard for me to imagine Rodrick in charge of anyone's safety.

One of the reasons I stopped swimming at the beach is because I got nervous the lifeguards weren't paying enough attention.

So whenever we'd go to the beach, I'd always introduce myself to them to make sure they knew my name and what I looked like. That way, I figured I had a better chance of getting rescued if I was struggling out there.

I'd even bring them snacks a few times a day, because you've gotta take care of the people who take care of YOU.

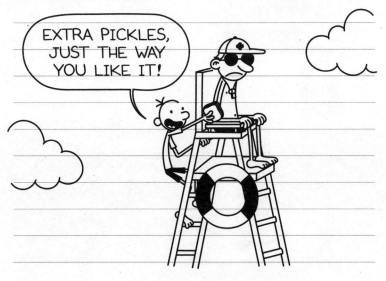

EXTRA PICKLES, JUST THE WAY YOU LIKE IT!

It's the same reason I never forget to send my pediatrician a Christmas card during the holidays.

I could tell the lifeguards at Ruttyneck Island were totally distracted with their phones. And if a rogue wave comes crashing to shore, I doubt they'd even NOTICE.

So I was happy to just lie under the umbrella and take it easy today. But there were these guys walking around the beach using metal detectors, which made it kind of hard to relax.

It made me think there could be pirate treasure buried a few feet beneath where I was sitting, and I felt like I should be DIGGING instead of taking it easy on my blanket.

I started imagining what it would be like to find a chest full of gold. You'd probably want to keep it a secret from everyone, or your friends and family would constantly be hitting you up for money, which could get annoying after a while.

But I'm guessing they'd figure it out anyway, because when you pay for everything in gold coins, people will start talking.

I actually have no idea what a single gold coin is worth, but it's gotta be worth a LOT, since gold is pretty rare.

Back in olden times, people used to pay for everything in gold and silver. But then some genius came up with the idea of printing PAPER money, and somehow they got everyone ELSE to go along with it.

One of these days, someone's gonna come up with a NEW form of money, and that'll replace the system we've got now. And I'm just hoping that someone is ME.

I've been testing the waters with a new monetary system I came up with last Christmas. I convinced Rowley that cucumber seeds were really valuable, and I traded a handful of them for his new video game controller.

Unfortunately, Mr. Jefferson found out about our trade and came down to my house to take Rowley's controller BACK. He never returned my seeds, though. So I'd better not see any cucumbers growing in the Jeffersons' garden this year or we're gonna have a difficult conversation.

I decided it wasn't worth going to the trouble of looking for buried treasure on the beach, though.

I figured if you start digging, you're just as likely to find a SKELETON as a treasure chest, and I'm sure the paperwork you have to file for that kind of thing is INSANE.

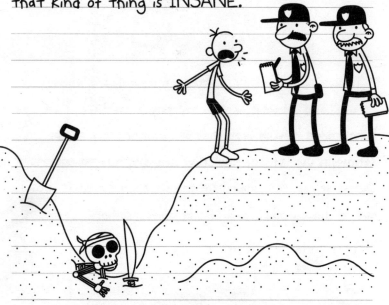

I felt kind of bad for Dad today, because he was the only person in our family who didn't get to relax. That's because he spent the whole afternoon going back and forth to the beach house, grabbing stuff people forgot to bring with them.

And after Dad went back to the house three times for Aunt Cakey, I realized she was messing with him for fun.

When Dad finally got a break, he took a tuna sandwich out of our cooler and sat down to eat it. But a seagull dive-bombed him and snatched it right out of his hand.

I've had issues with seagulls in the past, and I wasn't willing to let one steal my food.

So I took my sandwich with me to the bathhouse, which wasn't the best eating experience I've ever had.

I was pretty thirsty, so I planned on grabbing a bottle of water from our cooler. But the family on the blanket next to us was helping themselves to our drinks.

We confronted them about taking our water, but they said they thought the cooler was THEIRS. That wasn't very believable, though, since our name was written on the side.

Things got a little uncomfortable, so the other family packed up their stuff and left. I didn't want another family stealing our drinks, so I wrote something on the lid of the cooler with a marker to discourage anyone ELSE from opening it.

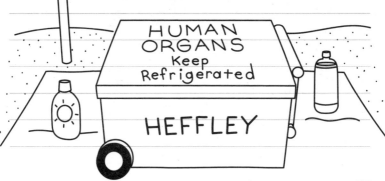

By that time, it was the middle of the afternoon and the sun was blazing. So Mom asked Dad to go back to the house and bring us another case of water to replace the bottles those people took.

I was glad Dad was getting more water, because it's important to stay hydrated.

My science teacher said the human body is 60% water, but that seems a little high to me. Because if people really WERE 60% water, we'd all look pretty freaky.

SPLISH

SPLOSH

But maybe he's right, and the reason old people are so wrinkly is that they're leaking really slowly.

In fact, I've made it my personal mission to keep my Great Uncle Colton hydrated, because he looks like he could be down to about 15% by now.

POUR

Dad got back with the case of water, and he also brought a big bag of beach toys Mom told him to fetch from the house. And even though I wasn't in the mood to break a sweat, this was one of those times when I could tell Mom wasn't gonna take no for an answer.

Mom pulled out all sorts of old-fashioned toys that she said used to keep her and her sisters busy for hours when THEY were kids. But people must've been wired a little different back then, because none of this stuff was doing anything for me.

The one toy that had some promise was a KITE, but it was too hard to steer it while watching where I was stepping.

And after making a bunch of people mad, I decided flying a kite wasn't worth the hassle. So I tied the string to the handle of the cooler and went back into relaxation mode.

But I must have dozed off and had no idea how much time went by. The thing that woke me was the ocean water soaking our beach blanket.

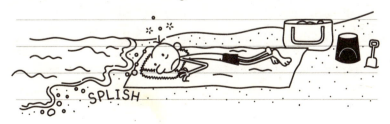

The tide was coming in fast, and my family wasn't anywhere to be found. So I had to gather up our stuff before everything washed out to sea. But that was easier said than done, especially without any help.

I was so focused on collecting our things that I wasn't thinking about what ELSE was in the water. And that's when I felt something disgusting attach itself to my leg.

I remembered Mom saying this island used to have a jellyfish problem, and I was POSITIVE that's what this thing was. But in my panic, I couldn't remember what you were supposed to do in the case of a jellyfish attack.

The best I could think of was to "stop, drop, and roll," so that's what I went with.

It turns out that what I THOUGHT was a jellyfish was actually just a clump of seaweed. And I guess the lifeguards were used to these kinds of false alarms, because nobody leapt to my rescue.

After I calmed down a little, I rinsed my leg off in the ocean. But I should've been paying better attention, because I got totally decked by a wave.

I dragged myself out of the water, and even though I was a little wobbly, at least I was out of danger. But now there was a pile of sand trapped in the netting of my bathing suit, and people were starting to NOTICE.

I couldn't just drop my drawers and flush out my bathing suit, so I moved to deeper water, where no one could see below my waist. I tried emptying out the netting, which wasn't easy to do, since I was fighting against the undertow.

All of a sudden, I had the lifeguard's attention. And from the way she reacted, she must've thought I was using the ocean as a toilet.

She tried to get me to come in to shore, but I wasn't budging. And I guess lifeguards must train for this sort of thing, because she hauled me to the shore in no time flat.

By that point, half our stuff had washed away and the rest was soaking wet. Luckily, the cooler didn't get swept away, so at least I had a place to sit and catch my breath.

I remembered there were still a few bottles of water in the cooler, and I pulled out the ones that were left.

But I didn't realize those water bottles were the only thing weighing the cooler down, and the kite yanked it clear off the ground.

I ran after the cooler, but it stayed just out of reach. And I might've actually caught up with it if there weren't so many obstacles in my way.

The cooler finally got wedged in some sand dunes, and I had a chance to grab it before it went airborne again.

But when I realized where I was standing, I decided maybe I should leave the cooler be.

I left the piping plover area as quick as I could, and luckily nobody saw me. Then I went back to our umbrella so I could get out of the sun. Because when it comes to protecting your skin, you can never be too careful.

<u>Monday</u>

When we got back to the beach house last night, all I wanted to do was jump in the shower. But we only have one bathroom for thirteen of us, and I had to wait my turn.

By the time I finally got in there, it was so steamy I could barely see. And it wasn't easy maneuvering between my aunts' wet bathing suits without touching anything.

My plan was to take a quick shower and get out.
But there was six inches of sludgy gray water in
the bathtub, and the drain was clogged with hair.

Worse than that, there was no hot water left,
so I had to take a cold shower. But I figured it
was worth it, because I wanted to feel clean and
fresh for when we went out to eat.

The only problem was that I couldn't get DRY.
Everyone had used up the towels, so I had to
use toilet paper to try and dab my skin.

It was taking way too long, so I tried shaking off, the way dogs do. But I couldn't really get the hang of it, and all I did was get water everywhere.

I guess I should've tried cleaning up after myself, because Aunt Cakey accused me of peeing on the toilet seat. So now there's a rule in the house that us guys have to sit down when we go to the bathroom.

Everyone was mad at everybody else for taking too long, so Mom created a bathroom schedule with fifteen-minute time slots. And I got the 6:30 p.m. shift.

I can't really control when I need to use the bathroom, though. And neither can Manny, who went out the window instead of waiting for his 9:30 p.m. shift to start.

SSPSSS

I decided I'd just use the bathroom at whatever restaurant we went to, because I figured they'd have a nice one there. And I was looking forward to getting a clean, warm towel to dry my hands.

But when I asked Mom where we were going for dinner, I got some very bad news.

Mom said we wouldn't be going out at ALL on this trip. She said that Gramma always made home-cooked meals on family vacations, and we were gonna carry on that tradition.

Personally, I think family traditions are a little overrated. Just because you do something once doesn't mean you should KEEP doing it.

The only tradition we've ever had is when Meemaw used to make everyone put their pants on their heads during Easter brunch. We all thought it was a little wacky, but Meemaw was raised in the Old Country, and we figured this was a custom where she grew up.

But after a while, Meemaw started doing OTHER goofy things, like wearing her underwear over her clothes, and we realized she was starting to lose her marbles.

I'm also not a big fan of eating together as a family. If cavemen clans ate at the same time, our ancestors never would've made it out of the Stone Age.

The other thing cavemen did right was that they only ate after a big hunt. And I'd much rather do it like THAT than have to eat three meals a day.

While I'm on the subject, there are a few other things I'd change around meals. First of all, I'd have a rule where no one is allowed to talk to you while you're eating, because my mom always decides to tell me the things I need to do when I'm in the middle of eating my cereal.

Plus, I don't like to be touched while I'm eating. I can totally understand why dogs snap at people who bother them while they're trying to enjoy their food.

Mom said we were gonna have spaghetti and garlic bread, and the grown-ups got to work making the meal. But the kitchen was tiny, and there were way too many bodies for such a tight space.

Plus, with a pot of water boiling on the stove and the oven going, it got super HOT in the kitchen. So everyone was all sweaty, even though we just showered.

Everybody had a different way of doing things, and different ideas about how to handle food. Aunt Audra accidentally spilled a whole box of spaghetti on the floor, so Mom said we were gonna have to throw it out.

But Aunt Gretchen said the boiling water would kill the germs from the floor, and Aunt Cakey agreed. That turned into a giant argument, and while that was happening, the garlic bread got burned.

Mom settled things by putting a NEW pot of water on the stove to boil, and said they could put the "floor noodles" in that one.

Aunt Cakey said the way you know spaghetti has been cooked long enough is by throwing it against the wall to see if it sticks. I don't think Mom was crazy about that approach, either, so she set up a third pot for the "wall noodles."

Mom and her sisters weren't the ONLY ones who had strong opinions about food. Vincent works in a fancy restaurant, and he kept testing the sauce to see if it needed any spices.

But Vincent kept putting the spoon in his mouth and then back in the pot, so I decided I'd skip the sauce.

Mom told me that Vincent is a "sommelier," which is a person who knows a lot about wine. She said when Vincent is testing a glass of wine, he takes a sip, swishes it in his mouth, and spits it out.

I had no idea there were people who do that kind of thing. And if you can get a job as a taco sommelier, I know exactly what I'M doing for a living.

Before the trip, Gramma cooked a batch of her meatballs and sent them along in a cooler.

But instead of putting all the meatballs in one big plastic bag, Gramma sent INDIVIDUAL bags for each person. And you knew exactly how much Gramma likes you by how many meatballs you got.

I felt bad for Vincent, who didn't get a bag, since he's not officially in the family. And I guess Aunt Cakey isn't the type of person who likes to share.

Aunt Audra didn't get any meatballs, either, but that's because she's a vegetarian. And if cows ever learn to speak English, I'm sure I'll become a vegetarian, too.

WHATCHYA GOT IN THE BAG, GREG?

Aunt Audra is real serious about healthy eating, and she always makes the rest of us read the labels on our packaged food. She says if you can't pronounce the ingredients, you shouldn't eat them.

BUTYLATED HYDROXYANISOLE...
PROPYLPARABEN...
MONOSODIUM GLUTAMATE...

Aunt Audra says that instead of listing the number of calories on the packaging of processed food, what they should REALLY do is tell you how much eating it will shorten your life. But if I knew that eating a candy bar would take three minutes off my life, I'm not sure I'd let that stop me.

After dinner was ready, we squeezed together at the kitchen table and ate our meal. Dinner conversation started off pleasant, but it went downhill pretty fast.

Aunt Gretchen talked about politics, and everybody had something to say. Thankfully, Mom stepped in before things went off the rails.

Mom started a list of "safe" topics that wouldn't cause any arguments, and everybody wrote one down on a piece of paper. And even though the topics were anonymous, it wasn't that hard to figure out which one came from Aunt Cakey.

Flowers	Romance Novels
Turtles	Pets
Television	Fashion
POP MUSIC	The time Susan stole Cakey's boyfriend when they were teenagers

Mom and Aunt Cakey launched right into a fight about something that happened the last time they came to Ruttyneck Island.

Apparently, Aunt Cakey was dating a lifeguard she met one summer, but then Mom snagged him for HERSELF. So I finally had an answer to the question of why Aunt Cakey and Mom don't get along.

Mom told Aunt Cakey that stuff happened a long time ago, and she should let it go. But I guess Aunt Cakey still hasn't gotten over it, even after all this time.

I could tell the conversation was making Dad uncomfortable. He didn't seem thrilled to be hearing a story about one of Mom's ex-boyfriends, and Vincent didn't look like he was enjoying the conversation that much, either.

Then Aunt Cakey accused Mom of stealing one of her meatballs, too. But Mom said Gramma put more meatballs in her bag, so that must mean she likes her BETTER.

The rest of us could tell this conversation wasn't going anywhere good, so we just started clearing the table.

Vincent volunteered to do the dishes, because apparently he's still trying to score points with our family. But if you ask me, he's wasting his time, because the only person he needs to impress is Gramma.

After dinner, everyone was happy to go their separate ways. But Mom wanted us to watch TV in the living room as a family. And even though it was a nice idea, getting twelve people and a dog to agree on what television show to watch is next to impossible.

Aunt Veronica wanted to watch a show called "The Great Cake Fakeout," which is a reality TV competition where these pastry chefs make cakes that look like regular objects, and then contestants have to guess which things are real and which are desserts.

But I'd be a terrible contestant on that show, because every time I think something's real, I'm wrong.

Mom vetoed watching that show, because it caused a lot of trouble in our house. When Manny saw it, he started thinking EVERYTHING was cake, which isn't OK when you're in a public restroom.

To make matters worse, now Manny's suspicious of REGULAR food, because he thinks it could be something else in disguise. So dinner takes twice as long, because Manny won't put anything in his mouth until Mom proves it's really food.

I can actually see how a person could start to get confused over what's real and what's not, because Rodrick's been messing with me for YEARS.

When I was little, Mom and Dad would sometimes put Rodrick in charge of my bedtime stories. One time, he told me that horses were imaginary creatures, like dragons or mermaids.

I was pretty sure I'd actually seen horses in real life, but Rodrick convinced me I'd just imagined it. So when I went on a field trip to a farm with my third-grade class, I was shook up when I came face-to-face with a real live horse.

I probably should've learned my lesson about trusting Rodrick by now, but every once in a while he gets me with something new. And when we went to the beach last summer, he sold me a can of shark repellent that was actually Mom's hair spray.

Since Mom vetoed the cake show, people started suggesting other things to watch.

Aunt Gretchen wanted to watch this series about a celebrity family who's always going from one crazy situation to the next. But Mom said those shows are as fake as the one with the cakes, and nothing that happens on them is actually REAL.

I don't know if she's right about that or not, but I'll bet those people who star in them are getting PAID. And I wouldn't mind faking things a little if we got good ratings.

If my family ever does get its own reality show, I've already got a name picked out for it.

HOUSE of HEFFLEY
Coming this fall

The reason it's never gonna happen is that my family's too BORING to have a show. And even though Rodrick got his lip stuck in the zipper of his coat once, it's not like you could base a whole episode on something like that.

What my family could use is a good SCANDAL. The thing that makes those reality shows interesting is that there's always some big secret, and it causes all sorts of drama. But if there's a juicy scandal in my family, everyone's done a good job keeping it under wraps.

Mom wanted to watch her favorite show, which is about the royals. And from what I've heard, that family knows a thing or two about drama.

The reason they're always dealing with problems is because the people who work for them leak their private business to reporters. And it must be hard to keep a secret when you've got inside information that somebody's willing to pay for.

But if I was actually a MEMBER of the royal family, it would be really tempting to cash in and spill the beans.

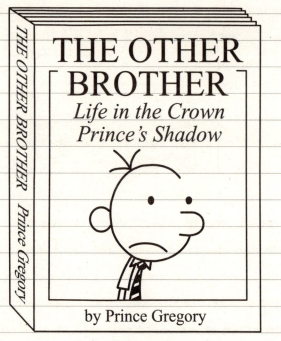

THE OTHER BROTHER

Life in the Crown Prince's Shadow

by Prince Gregory

When you're in a monarchy like those guys, there's a ton of pressure to get married and have kids to keep your bloodline going so you can stay in power.

But instead of going to all that trouble, it seems like it would be easier to just CLONE yourself instead.

I don't know if that kind of thing is even legal, but having another version of yourself would make dinner conversation a lot more satisfying.

It turns out that's not the way cloning works, though. I thought that when you cloned something, it was like making a COPY.

But my science teacher said that when you clone a person or an animal, it starts off as a BABY. And it would be a little weird changing your own diaper.

The one thing I can say about a monarchy is that those guys have clear rules about who's the next in line to the throne. But in my family, it hasn't been settled who's gonna take charge after Gramma is gone.

It feels to me like Mom should take over the family next, but her sisters probably aren't gonna let her without a fight.

All I know for sure is that it's gonna be a long time before MY generation is in charge. And if I ever get to be the head of the family, by then it probably won't be that much FUN.

Last night when we went to bed, it was still super hot in the house from the cooking, so I had a lot of trouble falling asleep. And when I turned on the ceiling fan to cool things down a little, I discovered that Vincent had hung his wet clothes on the blades to dry.

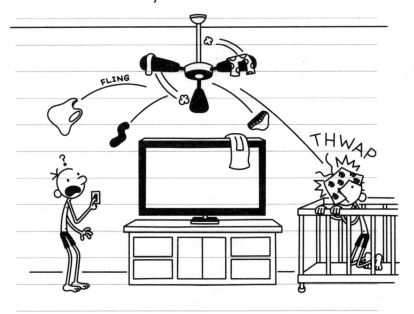

After I hung his clothes back up, I laid back down and finally fell asleep. But I wasn't out for long before a knock at the front door woke me up. I was nervous to answer it, because I couldn't imagine who would be knocking at that hour.

So when I saw a PIRATE standing on the front porch, I wasn't prepared.

It turns out the guy was actually Uncle Gary, my dad's younger brother, who was in a pirate costume.

I let Uncle Gary in the house, and he explained what he was doing here. This summer, he had been working at a baseball stadium, and his job was to go under the bleachers and find the stuff people dropped during the game.

But I guess he got hit on the head by one too many cell phones, and he decided it was time to look for a new line of work.

Uncle Gary said he wanted a job where he could be outside in the fresh air, and he started looking for opportunities at vacation spots. Then he found out there was an opening at a pirate-themed amusement park on Ruttyneck Island, which he visited with his family as a teenager.

JOB OPPORTUNITY

Skullduggery Cove is seeking an actor to perform as legendary pirate Wild William. Three performances on weekdays, five on weekends.

Before our trip, Mom told me how she and her sisters used to go to Skullduggery Cove when they were kids, and how scary it was to get chased by Wild William. And one time Aunt Gretchen got so scared she wet her pants.

According to Uncle Gary, the guy who had been playing Wild William had been in that role for thirty years, and he was finally retiring.

But it sounds like it ended badly for that guy, and it wasn't really his choice to call it quits.

Uncle Gary said that a few weeks ago, Wild William was chasing some kids in his rowboat, just like he'd been doing every summer for thirty years. But the kids he was chasing turned the tables on him and flipped his boat.

As if that wasn't bad enough, the manager at Skullduggery Cove told Wild William he couldn't tell kids he'd skin them alive anymore, because too many parents were complaining.

So the actor decided he'd had enough, and now he works at the fry shack on the boardwalk, where he has to wear a net over his beard so hair doesn't get in people's food.

Uncle Gary couldn't grow a decent beard, and he didn't want to show up for the job interview with a fake one. So he went to a hair salon and convinced them to sell him hair clippings.

Then he glued the clippings to his face and headed to Ruttyneck Island to apply for the job in a pirate costume. But he probably should've called ahead before just showing up, because when he got to Skullduggery Cove, the manager gave him some bad news.

She said that pirates aren't as popular with kids anymore, so the theme park decided to move in a different direction. The manager told him Skullduggery Cove was being rebranded as a butterfly sanctuary, and he should probably look for work somewhere else.

Uncle Gary said he didn't have enough cash to take the ferry back home, and he reached out to Dad to see if he could send him some money.

But when Dad didn't answer his texts, Uncle Gary looked up Dad's location on his phone and discovered he was right here on the island.

Uncle Gary said he needed to crash with us for the night. And even though I explained that there were no more beds, I guess pirates are used to sleeping in weird places.

This morning, I could tell Dad wasn't thrilled to see Uncle Gary at the kitchen table. And after Uncle Gary filled him in on everything he'd told me, Dad offered him money for a ferry ticket home.

But Uncle Gary said he wasn't in a big hurry to leave, and that he felt like he could use a vacation HIMSELF.

Mom seemed happy to have an extra person around to help carry our stuff down to the beach. But after what happened yesterday with the cooler, the beach was the LAST place I wanted to be.

I suggested we take a break from the beach and do something else instead. Other people must've been thinking the same thing, because everyone started jumping in with different suggestions for what we could do today. And Uncle Gary chimed in with a few thoughts of his own, even though he just got here.

Rodrick wanted to go to a record store, and Dad was hoping to go deep-sea fishing. Vincent wanted to take everyone to a cheese tasting, and the twins wanted to go to a "rage room," where you pay to destroy stuff.

Uncle Gary was pushing to go parasailing, and Aunt Audra wanted to go to a "sound healing" place, which seemed like the kind of thing a person like her does for fun.

But the idea I liked best was to have a spa day, which was Aunt Veronica's suggestion. I've let my toenails get a little long, and I thought it might be nice to have someone take care of that.

I think everyone would have been happy to split up and do our own thing, but Mom didn't like that idea. She said Gramma wanted us to do stuff together, so we needed to come up with something we could ALL do.

The only problem is that there aren't a whole lot of activities that work for a group with this age range. So we narrowed it down to mini-golf or a lighthouse tour, and I wasn't excited about either one.

First of all, if you've ever been mini-golfing with Manny, you'd know that it takes him FOREVER to get through a round. Everyone behind us gets annoyed at having to wait for him to line up his shots, which is really stressful.

And the last time we went mini-golfing, Manny won a free round by sinking a hole in one on the last hole, which meant we had to do it all OVER again.

But a lighthouse tour, which was Mom's idea,
sounded even WORSE. Whenever we go on
vacation, Mom always tries to squeeze in an
educational activity at a museum or historical site.

And I don't know how Mom finds these places,
but she always does.

Mom says kids have "brain drain" over summer
vacation, which is why she's always looking for
the opportunity to have us learn something. But
I PURPOSEFULLY put my brain in low-power
mode over the summer.

My theory is that if I learn too much during summer break, then I'll be ahead of my peers when we get back to school in the fall. Then I might be so smart I'll have to SKIP a grade, which seems like a bad idea to me, because I don't want to be the last one in my high school to get my driver's license.

I don't know what it is about guided tours and museums and stuff like that, but they suck the energy right out of my body.

In fact, last year, when my class went on a field trip to a paper mill, I had to take a three-hour nap after I got home to recover.

If I were a superhero, a museum would be like my kryptonite. And if a supervillain wanted to finish me off, all they'd have to do is take me to the still-life wing of an art gallery.

IF YOU LOOK CLOSELY AT THE BRUSH-STROKES, YOU CAN SEE THE WAY THE ARTIST WAS EXPERIMENTING WITH THE INTERACTION BETWEEN LIGHT AND COLOR.

NOOO! GASP!

To make it fair, Mom had everyone write down which activity they wanted to do, then put the slips of paper in a bowl. And even though I didn't really want to go mini-golfing, that's what I wrote down.

The only one who COULDN'T vote was Vincent, since he's not an official member of the family. And even though that might seem a little harsh, rules are rules.

The vote was split down the middle, with half the group voting for mini-golf and the other half voting for the lighthouse tour. But Rodrick hadn't voted yet, because he'd been in the bathroom.

Mom explained the two options to Rodrick and told him he was the deciding vote. But instead of just making a decision, he totally milked the situation.

Rodrick understood how much power he had, so he made people WORK to earn his vote. Each side tried to convince him to vote for their activity, but in the end it all came down to what people were willing to PAY.

The mini-golf people offered Rodrick half a bag of potato chips and a used Frisbee for his vote.

But the lighthouse group offered an unopened box of assorted saltwater taffy and an extra bathroom shift, so he took the deal. And if you ask me, it's not right that the other side won because they had deeper pockets.

We wasted too much time debating what we should do, though, because by the time we got to the lighthouse, there was a huge line.

I was sure the tour was going to sell out and we
were gonna end up going mini-golfing after all.
But then Mom bought tickets on her phone, which
was like cutting the line.

It turns out she snagged the last tickets for
the 10:00 a.m. tour, which made everyone who
had been waiting in line ahead of us MAD.

Rodrick saw an opportunity, and he sold his spot
on the tour to some random guy at the end of
the line.

I tried to sell MY ticket, but Mom stopped me before I could find a buyer. And even though I wasn't able to get out of the lighthouse tour, Rodrick gave me an idea I can use in FUTURE family get-togethers.

The next time we have a family gathering, I'm gonna PAY someone to take my place. Because there are a LOT of events I'd skip if I could, like random relatives' birthday parties and cousins' kindergarten graduations.

I guess I might have to pay extra for certain types of events, so I'll have to save up my money to get someone to sub for me on THOSE ones.

Our tour guide told us all about the history of the lighthouse and what it's like to be a lighthouse keeper, whose responsibility is to stop ships from crashing into the rocks at night. And even though it sounds like a pretty easy job, I'm sure I'd find a way to screw it up.

I figured the whole tour might take half an hour and then we could get on with our day. But the guy Rodrick sold his ticket to had a million questions, which our tour guide was happy to answer.

I'm sure Mom paid a lot of money for our tickets, but the people whose tickets we snatched from under them were listening in on our tour, even though they were pretending NOT to be.

I guess Mom was annoyed that this family was trying to get a free ride, so she made sure they couldn't hear what our guide was saying. And eventually they got the hint and left.

HEY HEY HEY!
WOO WOO WOO!

CLAP
CLAP
CLAP

By that point, I was eager to step inside to get out of the sun. But it was actually just as hot INSIDE as it was outside.

I thought there would be an elevator on the ground floor that would take us straight to the top, but we had to take the STAIRS. And we got jammed up, because the 9:30 group had wrapped up their tour and were trying to make their way back down to the bottom.

And with the heat and sweat and everyone's bodies pressed together, it was all a little too much for me.

By the time we finally made it to the top, I was
desperate for some fresh air.

After we spent a few minutes up there, the tour
guide said it was time to head back down. But
I wasn't planning on going ANYWHERE, and
nobody could make me, either.

Apparently, I wasn't the FIRST person to freak out in the middle of the lighthouse tour, and I guess the guides are used to dealing with this sort of thing.

After that experience, I'd be happy to never see another lighthouse as long as I live. But Mom spent a lot of time in the gift shop, so I have a feeling I know what everyone's getting for Christmas this year.

<u>Tuesday</u>
Tonight, I really wished we could've gone out to eat, but we had leftovers instead. Or at least MOST of us did. Apparently, Dazzle is too good for leftovers, and she refused to eat the reheated spaghetti.

So Vincent cooked a steak for Dazzle on the outdoor grill behind the house, then passed it through the bathroom window. And unfortunately, dinner was right in the middle of my shift.

I can understand where the dog's coming from on leftovers, because I'm not really a fan myself.

Lately, Mom's been cooking all our meals for the week on Sunday night, and by Wednesday or Thursday, we're having things for the second or third time around.

Then if there's any food left on Friday night, Mom mixes it together and serves it up like it's something new. And right before our trip, Mom took the leftover lasagna, meatloaf, squash, and taco salad from the week and put it all in the blender.

Some people say leftovers taste better than the original meal, but I'm just not one of them.

I don't think Dad's too crazy about leftovers, either, even though he'd never actually SAY it.

But I've noticed that Dad always seems to be late coming home from work on Friday nights, and I have a feeling that's no accident.

TRAFFIC WAS A NIGHTMARE!

After we were done cleaning up tonight, Mom wanted to play board games, just like her family used to do when they'd stay at the beach.

Everybody was still a little annoyed with Mom for coming up with the lighthouse tour, and nobody was really in the mood for any forced family fun. So most of us went into the living room to watch some mindless TV.

But Mom was already one step ahead of everybody else, because she had the remote.

We sat back down at the kitchen table, and Mom took some old board games out of a cabinet.

We started off playing a game where one person has to draw something on a piece of paper, and everyone else has to guess what it is. But the game ended in the first round after Malvin drew something rude.

Next, we played a game where one person is given a secret word, and they have to get their team members to guess it before the time is up.

The trick is that there are a bunch of OTHER words on the card that the player's not allowed to say, and if they DO, someone on the other team has to buzz them.

Things fell apart when people started using the buzzer for stuff that didn't have anything to do with the game. And when Aunt Cakey brought up the boyfriend Mom stole from her when they were teenagers, Mom used the buzzer to cut her off.

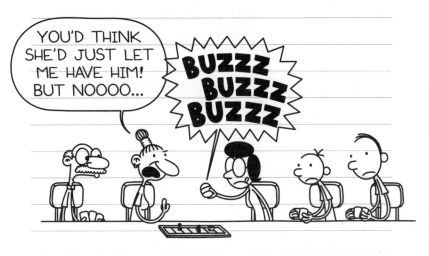

I was glad Mom interrupted Aunt Cakey, because the truth is that no kid really wants to hear about the people their parents used to date.

Mom pulled out another board game to keep things moving, and it was one I'd never seen before. The box was falling apart, and she was ready to put it away and reach for another game.

But Dad was excited, because it was a game he said he used to play with HIS family.

BOARDWALK BARON

It was called Boardwalk Baron, and Dad explained that the goal was to buy up properties and bankrupt all the other players.

Everybody seemed eager to give it a try except for Mom, who said a game like that taught people how to be GREEDY.

So Mom pulled out a different game where one player reads cards with interesting facts about marine animals.

Luckily, we still had the buzzer from that other game, and Rodrick wasn't shy about using it.

Everyone thought we should give Boardwalk Baron a try instead. But I guess Mom was pretty annoyed that she got overruled, so she said she was just gonna read in her room and then go to bed.

The rest of us opened up the box and got out all the pieces, and we ran into a problem right away. There weren't enough game tokens, and everyone started grabbing ones for themselves.

Uncle Gary managed to snag the cowboy hat, but I guess Manny really had his heart set on that one. So Manny swiped it and climbed on top of the kitchen cabinet until Uncle Gary finally agreed to just let him have it.

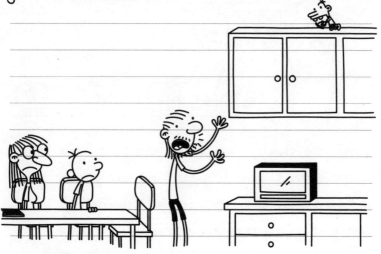

Malcolm and Malvin both wanted to be the wagon, so they decided to play as one team. I wasn't quick enough to get an official playing token, so I had to use a dirty coin from Aunt Gretchen's purse.

But anything was better than Uncle Gary's playing piece, which was a quarter of a meatball that someone found under the kitchen table.

Once everybody had their playing pieces sorted out, it was time to learn the RULES. But you practically had to have a college degree to understand the ins and outs of the game, so I figured I'd pick it up once we actually started to play.

IF A PLAYER ROLLS A NINE, BUT THE PRODUCT OF THE TWO DICE IS LESS THAN THE NUMBER OF HOTELS THEY HAVE ON THEIR MOST EXPENSIVE PROPERTY, THEN THE PLAYER MUST MOVE BACK THE NUMBER OF SPACES MATCHING THE SUM OF THE TWO DICE.

Everyone understood the basic idea, which was that the person who had all the properties at the end of the game was the winner, and they got named the Boardwalk Baron.

But everybody agreed there should be some sort of penalty for LOSING, so we started coming up with different ideas for punishments for the first person to go bankrupt.

Rodrick thought the loser should have to shave their eyebrows, but most of us thought that was too extreme. Uncle Gary said the loser should have to eat a gallon of mayonnaise, but that seemed kind of unsafe.

Then Aunt Cakey came up with an idea. She said that the loser should have to go out on the boardwalk the next day and sing until people passing by put twenty bucks in their hat.

Everybody thought that was a great punishment for being the first one to get knocked out of the game, because no one wanted to have to sing in public.

The only problem was that it made the game way too COMPETITIVE. Because once we started playing, everybody argued over every little thing.

On Aunt Gretchen's first roll of the game, one die landed on the table, and one landed on the floor, and that turned into a heated debate about whether or not her roll counted.

We finally agreed that both dice had to be on the table for a roll to count. Then on the very next turn, one of Rodrick's dice landed on the edge of the table, and we waited twenty minutes to make sure it didn't fall on the floor.

If you rolled double sixes, you landed in jail and had to sit out for two whole turns. But everybody felt like the punishment for landing in jail should be more serious than that.

So we turned the portable crib into a jail, and Aunt Veronica was the first one to land there.

The game was taking FOREVER, and everybody was getting pretty tired. Aunt Audra said she wanted to forfeit so she could go to bed, and we could split up her money and properties.

But everyone agreed that quitting was the same as going bankrupt. And I guess she really didn't want to have to sing on the boardwalk, so she made herself some coffee and powered through.

The twins were struggling, too, but they kept themselves in the game by taking turns napping.

The only person who was wide awake was Manny, and that's because he was WINNING. Somehow he had bought a whole row of properties without people noticing, and he was loading them up with hotels.

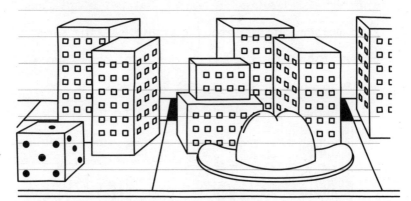

After a while, Manny had so many hotels on his properties that if someone landed on one, it would be game over for them. So he started charging people money to let them pass through his territory safely, and his fee wasn't CHEAP.

Eventually, everyone was almost out of money, and no one could afford what Manny was charging for safe passage anymore. So people started offering to go to jail just so they could sit out a few turns and not risk landing on one of Manny's properties. And before long, it was too crowded to fit anyone else in the crib.

The person who wanted to sing on the boardwalk the LEAST was Dad, so he tried to strike a deal with Manny. He promised he'd get him a bike for his birthday if he could pass through his properties safely the next round, but Manny was holding out for the cash up front.

Dad didn't have any cash on him, so he had no choice but to roll the dice. And when he did, he landed on the property where Manny had the most hotels, which meant Dad was TOAST.

I guess we were being a little too loud, because Mom came out of her bedroom. And she didn't look happy about being woken up.

With Dad out of the game, the rest of us started trying to figure out a good punishment for the SECOND-place loser. We decided it would be pretty funny if the person who went bankrupt NEXT had to dump a milkshake on their own head.

We couldn't decide if the milkshake should be chocolate or strawberry, so we asked Mom to settle it for us. But she decided we'd had enough fun for one night and announced that our game was officially OVER.

<u>Wednesday</u>
Even though Mom didn't seem to enjoy herself on
game night, the rest of us did. So this morning,
we asked her what she had in store for us NEXT.

But I guess Mom needed to take a break from
making plans for the family, and she said everybody
was on their own today.

I was pretty excited to have a day to myself,
but I wasn't sure what to DO. There was no
chance I was going to the beach, so I decided
I'd explore the town on my own.

But I was a little nervous about getting lost,
since I didn't really know my way around.

Mom told me she was gonna stay back at the house, and that I could take her phone as long as I was careful with it.

I knew it was a big deal for Mom to trust me with her phone, so I promised I wouldn't let anything happen to it.

It was a really hot and sticky day, and walking outside was like stepping into a sauna. So by the time I got to the boardwalk, my clothes were already soaked with sweat.

It was too hot to stay outdoors, and honestly I was looking for a way to avoid Dad anyway.

I went into a few stores that had air-conditioning, but it was pretty obvious that the employees who work at those places don't like it when people come inside just to cool down. And even though I pretended to be shopping, they weren't buying it.

I tried to find someplace cool where I didn't need to spend any MONEY, and I knew I'd found my spot when I stumbled across a library in the center of town.

I was a little nervous the people who worked there might ask me to leave, so when I sat in on an author's book talk, I made sure everyone knew I was paying attention.

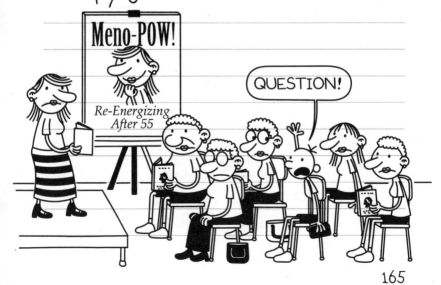

I wish I had remembered to put Mom's phone on silent mode, though, because it started dinging nonstop while the author was speaking. So I had to duck out into the hallway to see why I was getting so many alerts.

I was a little worried there was some kind of emergency and people were trying to reach me. But it was just my aunts sending texts on the family group chat.

Could someone get me an iced coffee if you're out and about?

You never paid me back for the one I got you last time.

That was two years ago Gretchen.

I've always wondered what kinds of things the grown-ups in my family talk about on that thread. But when I started scrolling through the old messages, I could see it was a bunch of nonsense.

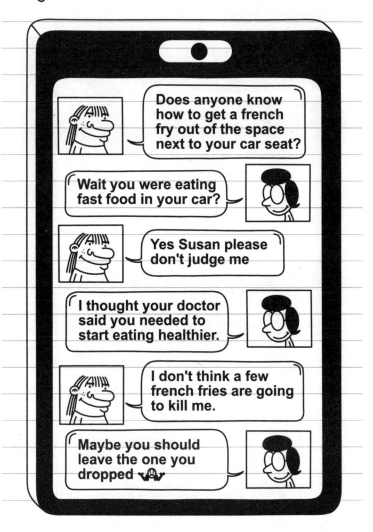

Every so often, someone would post something serious, like a medical question. And I really wish I hadn't gone looking through those old texts, because I saw some stuff on there I'd sure like to scrub from my brain.

But mostly the family group chat was just corny jokes and other stuff grown-ups must find funny.

I feel bad for Vincent because he's always asking to be added to the group chat, but he's not allowed since he's not a member of the family.

Now that I've actually seen the stuff people are posting, though, I can promise him he's not missing out on anything.

Besides, once you get on the family group chat, you can never get OFF.

Noah and Aunt Veronica broke up a couple of years ago, but he's still a part of the family thread. And I'm pretty sure the only reason he's still on it is because nobody can figure out how to REMOVE him.

So Noah's still getting updates on all the family news, even though it's clear that he wishes he WASN'T.

Even the DOG is on the family chat. And I can't tell if she writes her own texts or if someone does it for her.

I was thinking about how awesome it would be to become a social media star like Dazzle and have a whole team of people working for me. Then I realized I finally had a way to make that happen, because now I had a PHONE.

I started dreaming up ways I could start posting stuff and get a ton of people to follow me. But these days, EVERYBODY'S posting stuff online, and it's hard to stand out from the crowd.

At first I thought maybe I could just stream myself reviewing video games, but there are already a million people who do that kind of thing.

I decided that if I wanted to make a splash, I was gonna have to come up with something no one ELSE was doing. But you've gotta be creative if you're gonna carve out your own space.

I figured it would be smart to do product reviews so companies would send me free stuff. And I couldn't remember ever hearing about anyone who reviews PILLOWS before.

Plus, if I became a pillow influencer, I could literally make money in my SLEEP.

But I knew I wouldn't have my mom's phone for long, so I needed to come up with an idea where I could get a bunch of followers QUICK.

And that's when it hit me: There are a million ice cream shops on the island, so I could be a guy who samples all the different flavors and posts reviews online.

But there are lots of people who do that sort of thing, so I needed a gimmick to put me over the top. And when I finally landed on my idea, I knew it was a winner.

I realized that no one would want to watch a video of someone eating an entire ice cream cone, so I'd base my whole review on a single lick.

Now that I had a plan, I just needed to get started. So I went into an ice cream shop that was two doors down from the library and told them I was gonna need a few cones to review for my channel.

But the guy working there didn't seem to understand that social media influencers get free stuff, because he said if I wanted any ice cream, I was gonna have to PAY for it. And even after I explained that his store was about to miss out on some free publicity, he wouldn't budge.

So I walked out and went to another ice cream shop a block away, but they had the same response. And I was starting to wonder if these people understood anything about social media.

I finally found a place that was willing to give me a free sample on a tiny spoon. And even though I knew that wasn't gonna look as good on camera, I figured I had to start SOMEWHERE.

I posted my review, then waited to see what kind of response it got from people online.

But while I was waiting, I started worrying that maybe I wasn't thinking BIG enough with this One Lick Ice Cream Reviews idea.

I realized there are only so many flavors of ice cream out there, and eventually I was gonna run out of types to review. So I decided if I wanted my channel to GROW, I was gonna have to branch out with the sort of things I licked.

But that was a problem for another day, because right now my follower count wasn't where it needed to be.

**One Lick
Ice Cream
Reviews**

0
Followers

What I wanted was for some celebrity to follow my account, because then all THEIR fans would follow me. But I knew that was gonna be tough, because I don't really have any connections like that.

That's when I remembered that I DO know someone who's famous. And even though it's a DOG, it still counts.

DAZZLE

3.8 million
Followers

I thought about asking Aunt Veronica if she could get Dazzle to post something about One Lick Ice Cream Reviews on her channel. But then I remembered that social media influencers get PAID to do that kind of thing, and I probably couldn't afford whatever she charges.

That's when I realized I had something even BETTER, and it wouldn't cost me a dime. I found a picture on Mom's camera roll, and I cropped it.

Then I swapped it in as my new profile photo.

I didn't get the chance to see if the picture made a difference, though, because I wasn't looking where I was walking and I ended up wandering into somebody's front yard. And I guess the people who live on the island year-round don't like it when vacationers trespass on their property.

Getting blasted with a hose wasn't all bad, because after a day out in the heat, it was nice to finally cool off. But I learned a valuable lesson, which is that water and electronics don't mix.

<u>Thursday</u>
When I handed Mom her phone last night, the
first thing she did was put it in a bag of rice.
She said rice absorbs water, and it was the only
hope of getting the phone working again.

Even though I thought that sounded like a weird
thing to do, I was glad she wasn't too mad I
got her phone wet.

I think the reason Mom was willing to let it slide
today was because she was so busy trying to get
everybody ready for the family photo.

There was supposed to be a pretty sunset, and
she wanted to make sure everyone was showered
and looking nice for when we went down to the
beach after dinner.

The problem was that nobody remembered to pack a full set of white clothes, which Gramma asked everyone to wear for the family beach photo. But the stores were closing soon, and there wasn't enough time to go shopping AND make dinner.

So Aunt Gretchen came up with an idea. She said the adults could go clothes shopping while the KIDS made dinner. That sounded like a terrible idea to me, but for some reason all the grown-ups seemed to think we could handle it.

Once the adults were out the door, us kids were on our own. The first thing we did was open the fridge to see what we had to work with. I figured we could just reheat some spaghetti and call it a day, but Uncle Gary had eaten all the leftovers.

So we decided to make something new with the stuff that was in the fridge. The only problem was that there aren't a lot of meals you can make out of mayonnaise, salad dressing, and maple syrup.

That didn't seem to be a problem for the twins, though, because they were already off and running. They found some more food in the pantry and started mixing all the ingredients in a ceramic bowl. And if I hadn't kept an eye on them, Mom's phone would've ended up as part of their recipe.

I don't think Rodrick liked the look of what the twins were cooking up, because he found a frozen pizza in the freezer and put it in the oven.

Manny was doing his own thing, too. I guess he was in the mood for breakfast, because he started cooking up some pancakes, eggs, and bacon. But he was making a giant mess by cooking everything directly on the electric stovetop.

Speaking of MESSES, Malcolm and Malvin had gotten their hands on the electric mixer, which they totally lost control of.

In all the chaos, Rodrick accidentally turned the knob on the oven to "Self-Clean" instead of "Bake," so now the oven was heating up to nine hundred degrees.

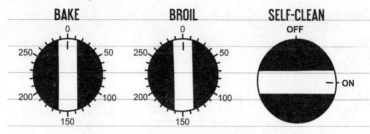

It turns out that once the self-cleaning cycle starts, you can't STOP it. So Rodrick's frozen pizza was getting incinerated inside the oven and there was nothing we could do about it.

Rodrick was worried we were gonna set off the smoke alarm, so he climbed up on a counter and fanned the fumes away from the detector.

And even though we managed to keep this from turning into something worse, I have a feeling that the grown-ups will think twice before putting kids in charge of the kitchen ever again.

One GOOD thing came out of the disaster, though. Since we used up all our food, Mom said our only choice was to go OUT to eat. And I'd been waiting to hear those words since we got here.

Of course, nothing's ever easy in my family, and people immediately started arguing over WHERE we should go to dinner.

Aunt Cakey was hoping to go to a seafood restaurant, but when Mom told everyone how a school of fish gobbled up people's throw-up on our ferry ride over, everybody suddenly lost their appetite for seafood.

Rodrick wanted to go to a restaurant called Jerks, where the waiters are mean to the customers. But nobody seemed wild about that idea, either.

Aunt Veronica pushed for going to a pet-friendly place where Dazzle could eat, but my family accidentally went to a place like that once, and it was no fun dealing with all the BEGGING.

It turns out we were wasting our time debating where to go, because every restaurant was totally booked except ONE. And that was a chain restaurant called Palazzo Pomodoro, whose commercials are always on TV.

I was kind of excited to try it out, and so were the other guys in the family. But Mom and her sisters were against it, because apparently Gramma HATES Palazzo Pomodoro.

Mom said that whenever a commercial for that restaurant comes on TV, Gramma complains that they use cheap ingredients and they don't know anything about authentic home-cooked food. Gramma even made Mom and her sisters promise never to eat there.

But the rest of us were STARVING, and we didn't really have any other options for eating. So Mom and her sisters agreed we could go to Palazzo Pomodoro as long as we all promised never to tell Gramma.

The plan was to take our family picture right after dinner, so everyone got dressed in our new white clothes. And I have to say it was a little embarrassing walking down the boardwalk looking like some boy band.

Even though Mom made a reservation on the phone ahead of time, the hostess said she couldn't find our names in the system. Then she told us we could wait for a table to open up, but that could take an hour or more.

So we sat in the lobby and tried to figure out what we should do. Mom was stressed because time was ticking away, and if we didn't eat soon, we wouldn't make it to the beach for the sunset. But if we tried to eat AFTER we took our picture, we'd never find a place that could take us.

Then Mom overheard the hostess talking to the manager about a large party who was a half hour late for their reservation. And that gave Aunt Cakey an IDEA.

The next thing I knew, Vincent was telling the hostess he was in the group that hadn't shown up. But I got the sense he wasn't super comfortable doing it.

It felt weird pretending to be a different family, but we couldn't let the reservation go to waste. So we all tried our best to get over it and just enjoy the experience.

After we had a few minutes to look over the menu, we placed our orders. Even though a restaurant like this is known for its pasta, I decided to go with the steak. And the only person to order spaghetti was Vincent, who was excited to finally have his very own meatballs.

The waiter came around with breadsticks, but this time I wasn't gonna fill up before my main course arrived. But somebody should've warned Dazzle about that, because she was making a rookie mistake.

Everybody was in a good mood, and for the first time I can remember, conversation was flowing. And I think maybe Aunt Cakey was having the most fun out of ANYONE.

She told Mom she was ready to forgive her for stealing her boyfriend all those years ago, and even though Mom seemed happy Aunt Cakey had turned a corner, I could tell she wasn't thrilled her sister was bringing up the topic again.

Then Uncle Gary said something I'll never forget as long as I live.

DID YOUR DAD EVER TELL YOU HE DATED YOUR AUNT CAKEY?

All this time, I never put it together that Aunt Cakey's ex-boyfriend was DAD. And the only person who took it harder than me was Rodrick, who had just taken a swig of iced tea.

Uncle Gary wasn't FINISHED, though. He told everyone the story of how Aunt Cakey met Dad when he was a lifeguard at Ruttyneck Island, and how they fell for each other. But when Aunt Cakey introduced Dad to the rest of her family, MOM liked him, too.

I guess Dad liked Mom better than Aunt Cakey, so then things got complicated. The two sisters fought over Dad, and Gramma had to step in and break it up.

Gramma could see that Mom and Dad were crazy about each other, so she decided they should be a couple. But to make things fair, Gramma told Mom she had to give Aunt Cakey her favorite sunglasses and a stuffed animal she'd won on the boardwalk.

And if you ever think it would be cool if YOUR family is hiding some big, juicy secret, all I can say is be careful what you wish for.

After Uncle Gary delivered his bombshell, nobody was really in the mood for conversation. So when our meal arrived, we ate in silence.

The only grown-up who didn't seem to know that Dad and Aunt Cakey had been a couple was Vincent, who seemed to have suddenly lost his appetite.

Aunt Veronica helped herself to one of Vincent's meatballs, and when she took a bite, you could tell something wasn't right.

Aunt Veronica passed Vincent's plate down the line, and before long everyone had a meatball in their mouth. And we were all thinking the same exact thing: These were GRAMMA'S meatballs.

That meant Palazzo Pomodoro had somehow gotten its hands on Gramma's secret recipe. Mom and her sisters started accusing one another of selling the recipe to the restaurant, but everyone denied they were the one who did it.

All at once they stormed the kitchen, and the rest of us followed them just to see what was gonna happen next. Then they confronted the chef and demanded to know where he kept the meatball recipe, but he played dumb.

196

That got the attention of the manager, who
threatened to call the cops if our family didn't
LEAVE.

In all the craziness, Dazzle saw her reflection in
a stainless steel refrigerator, and that's how she
found out she wasn't a person after all.

197

The manager chased us out of the kitchen, and we went back to the dining room. But the family whose dinner reservation we stole had finally arrived, and they were helping themselves to our food.

It was the same family from the lighthouse, and it only took a second for things to totally boil over.

Then the manager DID call the cops, and they came to the restaurant to calm things down. And it probably wasn't our best moment as a family.

The police took a report and interviewed everyone who was there. But Vincent denied knowing any of us, so they let him go. And at that point, you couldn't blame the guy for cutting bait.

The night wasn't OVER, though. After the police finished interviewing the other family, they let them go on their way. But when Mom gave the police her name for their report, they told us we were all going to have to join them down at the station, which freaked everybody out.

I had no idea why we were in more trouble than that other family, since they were just as much to blame for what happened as WE were. But when we got to the station, I knew exactly what this was all about.

As soon as I saw the cooler, I thought the police were gonna give us a hefty fine for trespassing in the piping plover habitat. But it turns out they were more concerned about the note I wrote on the lid about the human organs. So they stood back and made me open it to prove there was nothing too weird inside.

The cops seemed relieved that the only thing in the cooler were a few tuna sandwiches. And even though they were welcome to them, I'm just hoping no one gets sick.

Speaking of feeling sick, Mom was really upset that we didn't get our family photo before sunset. By now it was too dark outside to get a decent picture, and it was supposed to rain the next evening.

I guess the police felt sorry for Mom, because they offered to help us out. And even though it wasn't technically the photo Gramma asked for, it was the best we could do.

Ruttyneck Island
Police Department

Friday

Last night, when we got back to the beach house, all of Vincent's stuff was gone. Aunt Cakey was a little torn up about him leaving, but at least she had her sisters there to offer support.

I was looking forward to getting some sleep. But early this morning, I woke up to the sound of activity on our front porch, so I cracked the blinds to see what was going on.

I didn't know who all these people were, or if there was a parade planned on our street that day or WHAT, and I wished I could look it up. And that's when I remembered Mom's phone, which was still in the kitchen.

Believe it or not, Mom's trick actually WORKED and the phone turned on. When I saw the comments on my channel, I knew exactly what those people were doing on our front porch.

I have no idea how Dazzle's fans tracked her down to our house, but the only thing I knew for sure was that we couldn't STAY there. And once everyone else was awake and up to speed on the situation outside, they felt the same way.

So we packed up our stuff and slipped out the back window. And by then, nobody seemed to mind that we were cutting our vacation short.

Luckily, we were able to make it down to the pier without anyone spotting the dog. And on the way there we passed a lot of people who probably would've loved to get a selfie.

The next ferry wasn't for two more hours, so we had to hire a boat to take us back to the mainland. And even though I wasn't crazy about the TYPE of boat we got, I knew there was no point in making a stink about it.

Everyone was relieved when we got to shore. But that's when we found out Dazzle had somehow given us the slip back on the island.

I guess Dazzle decided she'd had enough of our family, and I could totally relate. Because I was looking forward to taking a break from these people MYSELF.

Aunt Veronica called the police station at Ruttyneck Island and told them about her missing dog, and they said they'd get the word out. And while we were waiting to hear back, Mom had an idea.

Today was Gramma's seventy-fifth birthday, and Mom thought it would be fun to surprise her at the assisted living center.

Everybody thought that was a good idea, so we formed a caravan of cars and drove to Gramma's new place.

But the security at Gramma's complex is pretty tight, and the guy at the gate wouldn't let us in until he contacted Gramma and got her permission for us to be on the property.

He called her apartment, but she didn't pick up. So he told us we'd have to come back another day.

At that point, nothing was stopping my mom and her sisters from seeing Gramma on her seventy-fifth birthday. So they decided we'd SNEAK onto the property by going around back.

And even though everybody understood that what we were doing was trespassing, it didn't come close to the worst thing we'd done on this vacation.

We snuck inside Gramma's building through a rear entrance and took the stairs up to her apartment. But when we knocked on her door, there was no answer.

KNOCK
KNOCK
KNOCK

By now, everyone was getting pretty concerned, and Mom decided we were gonna have to go back to the gate and tell the security guard that we needed him to let us inside Gramma's apartment to check on her.

Everybody knew that would probably get us in trouble, but we all agreed it would be worth it to know Gramma was OK.

So we took the elevator down to the first floor and headed for the front door. But on the way there we noticed loud music coming from the rec center, which was PACKED.

I figured somebody must be having a party in there, and when we poked our heads in the door, I found out I was RIGHT.

It was bad enough that Gramma had her birthday party without us. But what made it sting a little EXTRA was seeing all these strangers helping themselves to her famous meatballs.

CHEW   MUNCH   SMACK   SLORP

It took a while for the party to wind down, and once the room finally cleared out, Mom and her sisters got some time alone with the birthday girl.

Gramma started off by apologizing for not inviting everyone to her seventy-fifth birthday party. She said she felt bad about sending us all away, but this year she just didn't want to deal with any family drama.

And after spending almost a whole week with everyone, I can confirm that Gramma made the right call.

I think it's crazy that she sent us all off on a vacation nobody wanted to go on to buy herself a little personal space. But that goes to show how much power you have when you're the head of a family.

Speaking of power, Gramma told everyone we needed to help clean up the rec center. And it sure would've been nice to have Vincent around right about then.

I felt bad about what happened with him, but it turns out he's doing just fine.

In fact, he sent everyone a text message on the family group chat, which the dog must've invited him to join.

After everything that's happened over the past few days, I didn't think anything could shock me anymore. But there was still one big surprise left.

Gramma asked me to take the trash out to the dumpster, but the bag was a lot heavier than I thought, and it burst open.

When I started picking up the trash that spilled, the label on a plastic bag caught my eye.

And just like that, everything was suddenly clear. Palazzo Pomodoro didn't steal Gramma's meatball recipe after all. This whole time, she's been buying her meatballs from THEM.

That explained why Gramma made her daughters promise to never eat there. She knew that if the family found out her secret, her power would go up in smoke.

So when Gramma saw me standing there holding the empty bag, she froze. And for a second, neither one of us knew what to say.

I thought about telling everyone in the family that Gramma's meatballs were store-bought and we could just order them whenever we wanted.

But then I had ANOTHER thought. If I kept Gramma's secret to myself, maybe I could be the next head of the family. And then I'D be the guy calling the shots about where everyone goes on vacation and who gets to marry who.

So I promised Gramma her secret was safe with me, which puts me in a position to take over the family when the time comes. And even though I feel bad about cutting the line, when it comes to power, sometimes things can get a little messy.

ACKNOWLEDGMENTS

Thanks to my dad for fostering a love of comics, introducing me to Carl Barks and starting me on a journey to become a cartoonist. Thanks to my mom for your love and encouragement throughout my life. Thanks to my wife, Julie, for being so patient and supportive during the deadline grind.

Thanks to Charlie Kochman for applying the skills you've developed in a career in comics, helping so many cartoonists create their best work.

Thanks to the Wimpy Kid team—Anna Cesary, Vanessa Jedrej, Shaelyn Germain-Dupre, and Colleen Regan—for your enthusiasm and professionalism.

Thanks to everyone at Abrams, especially Mary McAveney, Andrew Smith, Melanie Chang, Kim Lauber, Alison Gervais, Erin Vandeveer, Borana Greku, Pamela Notorantonio, Lora Grisafi, Mary Marolla, and Talia Behrend-Wilcox. Thanks to Mary O'Mara for being such a steady hand at the wheel. Thanks to Steve Roman for your attention to detail.

Thanks to the wonderful team at An Unlikely Story. Thanks to Rich Carr, Andrea Lucey, Paul Sennott, Sylvie Rabineau, and Keith Fleer.

Thanks to everyone at Disney, especially Roland Poindexter, Kathryn Jones, and Vanessa Morrison.

ABOUT THE AUTHOR

Jeff Kinney is a #1 *New York Times* bestselling author, a six-time Nickelodeon Kids' Choice Award winner for Favorite Book, and one of *Time* magazine's 100 Most Influential People in the World. He spent his childhood in the Washington, D.C., area and later moved to New England, where he and his family own a bookstore called An Unlikely Story.